Shadow &

A Game of Hide-and-Seek

By: Patricia Morrison

Illustrated by: Samuel Batley

Shadow & Us: A Game of Hide-and-Seek

First Printed in United Kingdom 2021

Published by Conscious Dreams Publishing
www.consciousdreamspublishing.com

Edited by Rhoda Molife
www.molahmedia.com

Illustrated by Samuel Batley
Typeset by Shabana Asif

ISBN: 978-1-913674-67-0

Dedication

I dedicate this book to my four beautiful and kind-hearted children who give me a reason to get up every day, to strive to give them the best possible life and to be an inspiration for them.

Chapter 1

One bright sunny afternoon, sisters Kacey and Kayla were playing in their front garden while their mother was cooking and keeping an eye on them through the kitchen window.

They had just finished playing hopscotch then Kacey shouted, "I know what we can do! Let's do some handstands!"

So up and down they went.

"Up together, down together, 1,2,3 together," they sang happily.

After a few minutes, little sister Kayla declared, "I'm tired. Can we get a drink?"

Big sister Kacey went inside to get some juice while Kayla sat down on a little step, listening to the sweet breeze whistling through the trees.

Suddenly, Kayla heard a voice whispering, "Come on. Let's play."

She looked up and saw a shadow against the wall.

"That was quick!" Kayla said as she turned to grab the drink from who she thought was Kacey.
To her surprise, Kacey wasn't there. Kayla was puzzled and scratched her head.

"Hmm," she muttered.

She looked at the wall again and the shadow was still there.

Kayla whispered, "Who are you then?"

To Kayla's surprise, the shadow replied, "I'm your sister's shadow and I've been watching you play all day. You were having so much fun. I really want to play with you two. Can I play with you?"

Kayla, who always liked an adventure, did not hesitate and replied, "Wow! OK! This is going to be fun. Let me get my sister."

With that, Kayla jumped up and ran into the kitchen to tell Kacey about the talking shadow on the wall!

Chapter 2

"Kacey! Guess what? Someone wants to play with us, and you wouldn't believe who it is!" squealed Kayla with excitement.

"Who is it?" asked Kacey.

"It's your shadow!" replied Kayla.

"Really? My shadow? Let me see!" shouted Kacey.

Drinks forgotten, the sisters ran outside.

"There she is!" shouted Kayla.

Kacey's shadow jumped up all set to play. Kacey couldn't believe her eyes, which were now as big as saucers.

"Is... this... real?" Kacey asked slowly, rubbing her eyes before taking another good look at the wall. "Wow! This is this real."

"I told you! I told you!" laughed Kayla. "So what

are we going to play?" she continued. "Let me see...," mumbled Kacey's shadow, rubbing her chin. "I know! Let's play hide-and-seek!"

"We love hide-and-seek," squealed Kayla and Kacey in unison. They often spoke at the same time.

Kacey said she would count so Kayla and Kacey's shadow scattered away in the garden to hide. Kacey covered her eyes and started counting.

"1, 2, 3, 4, 5..." After stopping at 20, she shouted out really loudly, "Ready or not, here I come!"

When she opened her eyes, the garden was empty and quiet. Kacey started her hunt and first ran over to the shed. No one was there. So, she ran over to the tree house quietly climbed up the ladder and peeked inside. There, in the corner, was a pink bow sticking out from behind the small bookshelf.

Kacey tiptoed over very quietly trying not to make the floorboards squeak. She crawled behind the bookshelf, right behind Kayla. Then she tapped her on her shoulder.

"Boo!" said Kacey.

"Ahhh!" screamed Kayla, as she jumped up in fright.

She then toppled over backwards, falling on top of Kacey with a crash. They both rolled around on the floor giggling.

"Right! You need to find your shadow now Kacey," said Kayla.

"OK! Let's go. She's going to be hard to find so you need to help me Kayla," replied Kacey.

The sisters climbed down the ladder of the treehouse and set off to find Kacey's shadow.

Chapter 3

They jumped off the bottom of the ladder one by one, then ran around to the front garden. Kayla spotted a shadow on one of the bins then turned to Kacey with her fingers on her lips, pointing to the bin. Kacey responded by putting her fingers on her lips too, and they both quietly tiptoed towards the shadow.

"Boo!" Kacey shouted, as she touched her shadow. Kacey's shadow jumped and all the bins toppled over with a big bang, giving everyone a fright. Before they knew it, Kacey and Kayla's mother was right next to them, wondering what all the noise was about.

"What's going on out here? Are you girls OK?" asked their mother. "And why are the bins all over the place?"

"It wasn't us Mum. It was the shadow!" Kayla replied quickly.

"What shadow?" their mother asked with a puzzled look.

The sisters both pointed at the shadow which was now on the fence next to the bins. The shadow pointed back at them. Kacey was confused.

"Why are you copying me? Tell Mum it was you!" demanded Kacey.

Kacey's shadow remained silent. Then Kacey put her hand on her head and to her surprise her shadow copied her and put her hand on her head too.

Their mother picked up the bins, shook her head and went back inside. As soon as the front door shut, Kacey's shadow sister came back to life.

"Boo!" she shouted.

"Ahhhh!" screamed Kacey and Kayla.

"Why didn't you tell Mum that it was you?" asked Kayla.

"Well you're the only ones that can hear me. That's because you have playful minds which grown-ups don't have. That's only for little people like us. They used to though when they were little. When you are like us, things that don't look real to grown-ups come to life for us. Like me! It's so much fun."

"So this is like our little secret," smiled Kayla.

"That makes it even more fun," Kacey said. "Well, let's play another round!"

They all ran to the back garden to start round two of hide-and-seek.

"I can count this time and I'll find you two. But... I think I'll need some help" said Kacey's shadow mysteriously.

"Help? Help from who?" replied Kacey and Kayla at the same time.

"Well! Guess what? I have a little sister too! She's the exact same height as you Kayla and she's wearing a dress just like yours," giggled Kacey's shadow.

"No way! Where is she?" Kayla asked.

"Turn around and look next to you on that fence over there. She's been following you around all day," giggled Kacey's shadow.

Kayla turned towards the fence to face her shadow. Without hesitation, she said, "Hello my shadow. I'm Kayla and this is my big sister Kacey."

Kayla's shadow jumped up and down with excitement and squealed back, "Hi Kayla! Hi Kacey! I can't wait to play with you. I'm so excited. I've been following you around all day hoping you will ask me to play!"

"I'm really sorry I didn't see you. I've been having so much fun with these two," replied Kayla.

Kacey and Kayla looked at each other with great, big grins on their faces.

Chapter 4

"You two go and hide and my big shadow sister and I will come and find you," instructed Kayla's shadow.

They both started to count while Kacey and Kayla scattered off to hide.

"1, 2, 3, 4, 5...," the shadow sisters counted in unison all the way to 20. "Ready or not, here we come!"

They started their hunt, looking all around the garden.

On the way to find the girls, Kacey's shadow sneaked in a cheeky go down the slide.

When she got to the bottom of the slide, she could see two feet poking out between the wall and shed. She walked quickly to the shed, popped her head round and shouted, "Boo! I've found you Kayla!"

"Oh no! You found me first. This is my best hiding place and I thought you would never find me here!"

Kayla got up and followed the shadow sisters across the garden as they set off to find Kacey.

"Hey! Come over here," whispered Kacey's shadow. "I think I heard Kacey in the treehouse."

Kayla and her shadow followed Kacey's shadow to the treehouse and one by one, they crept up the ladder into the treehouse. As Kayla crawled in last, she spotted Kacey's eye peeping through the curtain. Kacey quickly put her finger on her lips to make sure Kayla didn't blow her cover to the shadow sisters.

Kayla smiled and told the shadow sisters to check behind the bookshelf. "That's her favourite hiding spot," she told them.

The shadow sisters crept over to the bookshelf hoping to scare Kacey. Kacey's shadow jumped round the back of the bookshelf and Kayla's shadow popped her head over the top.

"Boo!" they both shouted, only to realise that Kacey wasn't even there.

"Where could she be?" moaned Kayla's shadow with her hands on her hips.

Chapter 5

Kayla started giggling.

"What's so funny?" asked the shadow sisters; they too often spoke together.

"Err..., nothing," replied Kayla, while pretending to look out the window.

Kacey's shadow could see that Kayla was actually looking at the curtains and not out of the window. "Ah ha!" she said. "I bet I know where she is!"

Kacey's shadow went over to the curtain, reached out and started to tickle and tickle and tickle the curtains.

Of course, Kacey started laughing and soon she collapsed to the floor in a fit of giggles.

"I got ya! I got ya!" shouted Kacey's shadow.

"Yes, you did, but I'm still the winner!" replied Kacey while hugging Kayla.

Kayla suddenly remembered she was still thirsty. "Oh Kacey! How silly of us! We left our drinks in the kitchen."

"Oh yeah! Come on, let's go get them and we can come out and play some more with our shadows," replied Kacey. "Do you want to come with us shadow sisters?" she asked the shadows.

"Yes, we would love to. But remember, your mum won't be able to see us," said Kacey's sister.

"That's OK. We'll bring you a drink outside."

One by one, they carefully went down the ladder. As they walked over to the house, they saw Kacey and Kayla's mum knocking on the window and shouting out loudly to them.

"It's time to come in for dinner girls!"

"Aww! Noo!" Kacey and Kayla cried. They weren't happy at all.

"Wish we'd stayed in the tree house now. I don't want to go inside! Plus, I'm not even hungry yet," said Kayla crossing her arms and frowning at the window.

They'd had so much fun and they didn't want it to end. Kacey knew though that they had to do as their mother said.

"Ah well," Kacey sighed. "We have to go now."

"I hope we can play again together soon," said Kacey's shadow.

"Of course you can. Next time, you can come to the park with us," Kayla promised the shadow sisters.

And so, Kacey and Kayla waved goodbye to their shadow sisters. As they ran up the garden to the house, Kayla said to Kacey, "I wonder what game we can play with our shadows next time..."

About the Author

Patricia Morrison is a payroll officer and childminder based in Manchester. She is married with four children. With her husband, she also runs a Saturday football academy.

Shadow & Us: A Game of Hide-and-Seek is her first book which she wrote whilst on furlough during the COVID-19 pandemic of 2019-2021. She was largely inspired by her daughters' YouTube short film called Shadow & Us, as well as by the imaginative play of the children she looked after as a childminder.

This is her first book.

YouTube: Cool Sisters22
Tiktok: @justtrisha6

Q&A with the Author

What inspired you to write Shadow & Us?

I was inspired to write this book by my two lovely and creative daughters, Shalece and Shamiah. They have a YouTube channel that features short films and music videos. Their imaginative stories brought out my creative side, especially as I had more time on my hands. You see, I had been furloughed during the COVID-19 lockdown and up until that time, I had been caught up in home life with my husband, four children and work.

How did you get started with the book?

I was amazed at how much of myself I had hidden away. First, I started drawing. Then I opened a TikTok account to share my work. The first picture I posted received 600 views. I then started writing a story based on some videos my girls and I had made a few summers back about their shadows. It wasn't my intention to write a book though; I just wanted to do something different.

After telling a friend about the story I had written, I jokingly said, "Hey, I could turn this into a book." My friend replied, very seriously, "Why not?" I just laughed it off, but she didn't stop. "Why laugh? Of course you can!" My first thought was, Me... no way could I even do that. I can't and I'm rubbish at English anyway and I wouldn't even know where to start.

Over the next few weeks, I couldn't get the idea out of my head, so I gave myself a good talking to about doing something with what I'd written. I went to good old Google and searched for 'how to publish a book.' I found a few publishing companies, had a few calls but none really sold themselves to me or were just super expensive. What I did learn was that I would need an illustrator, so off I went to look for one.

Who helped you create the book?

I came across Samuel Batley who was very encouraging, so I shared my story with him. He sent me some sample illustrations which my girls and I were happy with. Then I sent everything off to a publishing company I had finally chosen. However, I just didn't feel that there was a connection between us; to me they were more interested in the drawings and not the story. I tried a few more publishers and had a few offers but none really stood out for me.

Then I thought about self-publishing. I set up an account with Amazon but didn't do anything with it. I guess I wasn't feeling confident about the whole thing as it seemed so hard to me. Then out of the blue, I received an email from an enquiry I'd made to Conscious Dreams Publishing saying they were ready for me to submit my manuscript. I thought, Why not? So, I did. They were happy with my story. We exchanged a few emails and they were very helpful and patient with my questions. When I decided to work with them, I knew it was the right decision. It felt as if they'd chosen me rather than me choosing them.

What advice would you give to someone who wants to start their own exciting new project?

So with this book, I would encourage anyone who wants a change or to start something new to simply go for it. You will rediscover hidden talents, learn new skills and regain your confidence. I did and here I am... a published author!

Acknowledgements

To my daughters – thank you for creating the characters and storyline for this book.

To my friend Caroline Moon – thank you for encouraging me to believe in myself.

To Simon Batley – thank you for bringing the book to life with your amazing illustrations.

To Daniella Blechner of Conscious Dreams Publishing and Rhoda Molife, Editor at Molah Media – thank you for bringing my book up to the high professional standard I wanted.

To the children I work with every day – thank you for bringing your imaginations to life and inspiring me.

Conscious Dreams
PUBLISHING

Be the author of your own destiny

www.consciousdreamspublishing.com

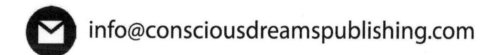
info@consciousdreamspublishing.com

Let's connect